Copyright © 2020 John and Eveline Clark.

Illustrations by John Clark.

All rights reserved. No part of this book may be used or reproduced by any means, graphic, electronic, or mechanical, including photocopying, recording, taping or by any information storage retrieval system without the written permission of the author except in the case of brief quotations embodied in critical articles and reviews.

Archway Publishing books may be ordered through booksellers or by contacting:

Archway Publishing
1663 Liberty Drive
Bloomington, IN 47403
www.archwaypublishing.com
1 (888) 242-5904

Because of the dynamic nature of the Internet, any web addresses or links contained in this book may have changed since publication and may no longer be valid. The views expressed in this work are solely those of the author and do not necessarily reflect the views of the publisher, and the publisher hereby disclaims any responsibility for them.

Any people depicted in stock imagery provided by Getty Images are models, and such images are being used for illustrative purposes only. Certain stock imagery © Getty Images.

ISBN: 978-1-4808-8810-4 (sc)
ISBN: 978-1-4808-8809-8 (e)

Library of Congress Control Number: 2020909079

Print information available on the last page.

Archway Publishing rev. date: 06/15/2020

The Monk and the Dragon

for Eveline

Once, high atop a cold and distant mountain, deep within a cave, there lived a small, quiet, and simple monk.

He was by nature a serious sort, though peaceful, and he went about his days on the mountain in a thick, pale robe, alone and without any fuss.

The monk led a life of humble meditation, apart from any monastery, and notable for being serene, disciplined, virtuous, and fulfilled.

However, if he were to be truly honest with himself (and he was always honest with himself), the monk had come to realize that somehow he'd grown listless.

One day an immense dragon flew over the mountain and alighted upon the broad stoop of the cave.

The dragon was a terrible creature to behold — darkly beautiful, with crimson opaline scales, slender ebony spines, luminous hazel eyes, and all smelling of flint and ash.

She bore many a scar owing to the sling, the arrow, and the sword, and indeed that day she had been freshly wounded.

The dragon was angry and bitter from the ceaseless attacks upon her wherever she went, and she was looking for a safe place to rest.

Upon seeing the monk, the dragon scowled, bared her fangs, and prepared to breathe fire.

Upon seeing the dragon, the monk was horrified and began to retreat slowly into his cave.

Yet as they caught each other's gaze, the moment of confrontation gently suspended itself.

It was then that something profound quietly became manifest and delicately began to unfold.

T he monk's fear eased and gave way to a fascination with the exotic creature arrayed before him.

He found himself captivated by the dragon's beauty and equally by the sadness he sensed in her exasperation.

The dragon, for her part, discovered herself tempered by the monk's placid demeanor and calmed by the unaccustomed kindness in his eyes.

Moved by the dreadful story told in the dragon's wounds, the monk took a tentative step toward her.

The dragon, with a surprising sense of relief, warily permitted his approach.

Once at her side, the monk lightly reached up to her with his hand, and the dragon ... she gingerly lowered her head.

With their touch, calloused hand to gleaming scale, there was born a deep, unspoken, and timeless understanding.

"I am bored and lonely on my mountain," confessed the monk.

"I've become weary of the world and have been forsaken by it," said the dragon.

"I envy you your travels and all the things you have seen," admitted the monk.

"I long for your high mountain and your safe cave," replied the dragon.

At that there was a pause in the conversation as each considered what the other had revealed.

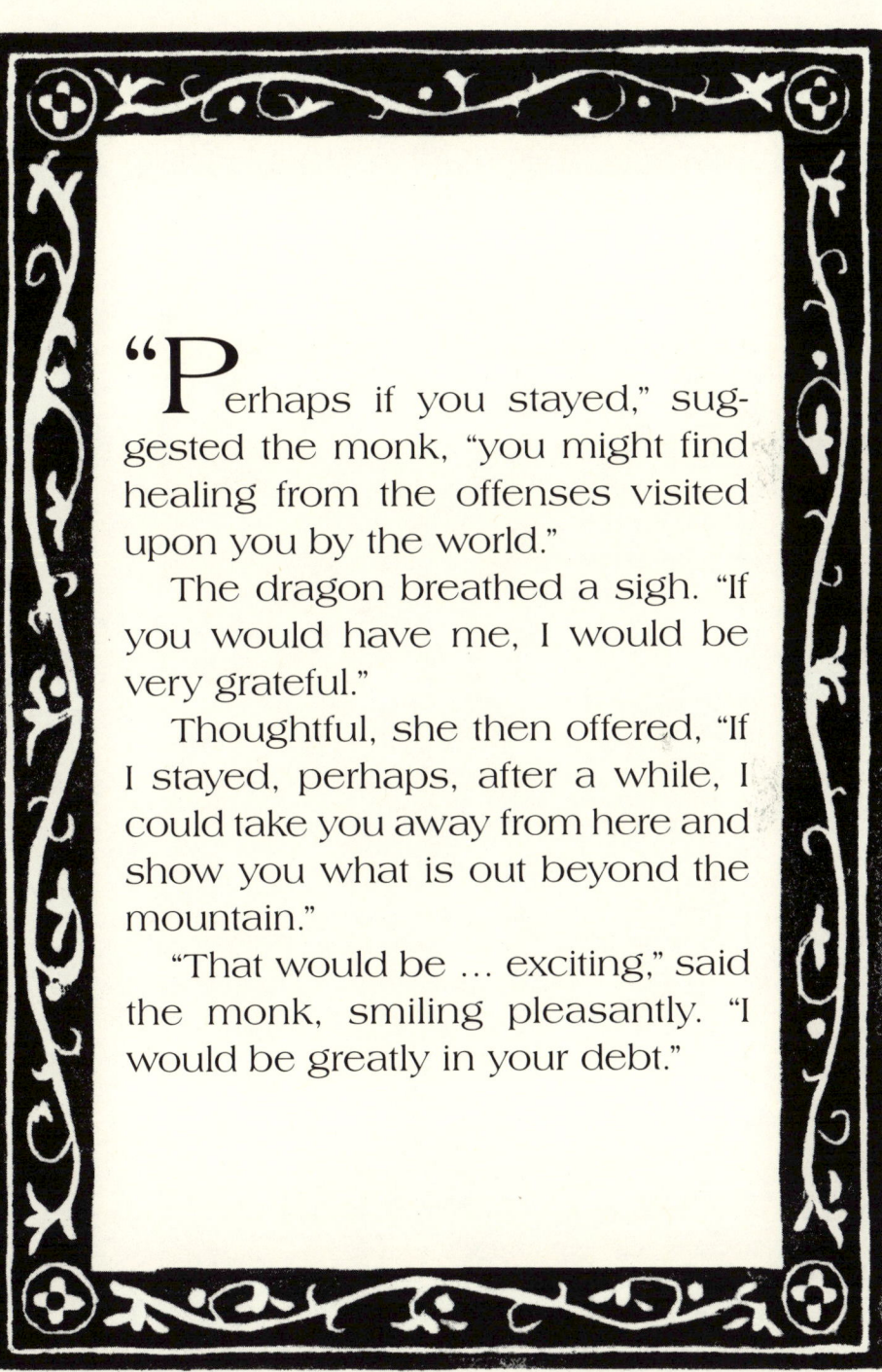

"Perhaps if you stayed," suggested the monk, "you might find healing from the offenses visited upon you by the world."

The dragon breathed a sigh. "If you would have me, I would be very grateful."

Thoughtful, she then offered, "If I stayed, perhaps, after a while, I could take you away from here and show you what is out beyond the mountain."

"That would be ... exciting," said the monk, smiling pleasantly. "I would be greatly in your debt."

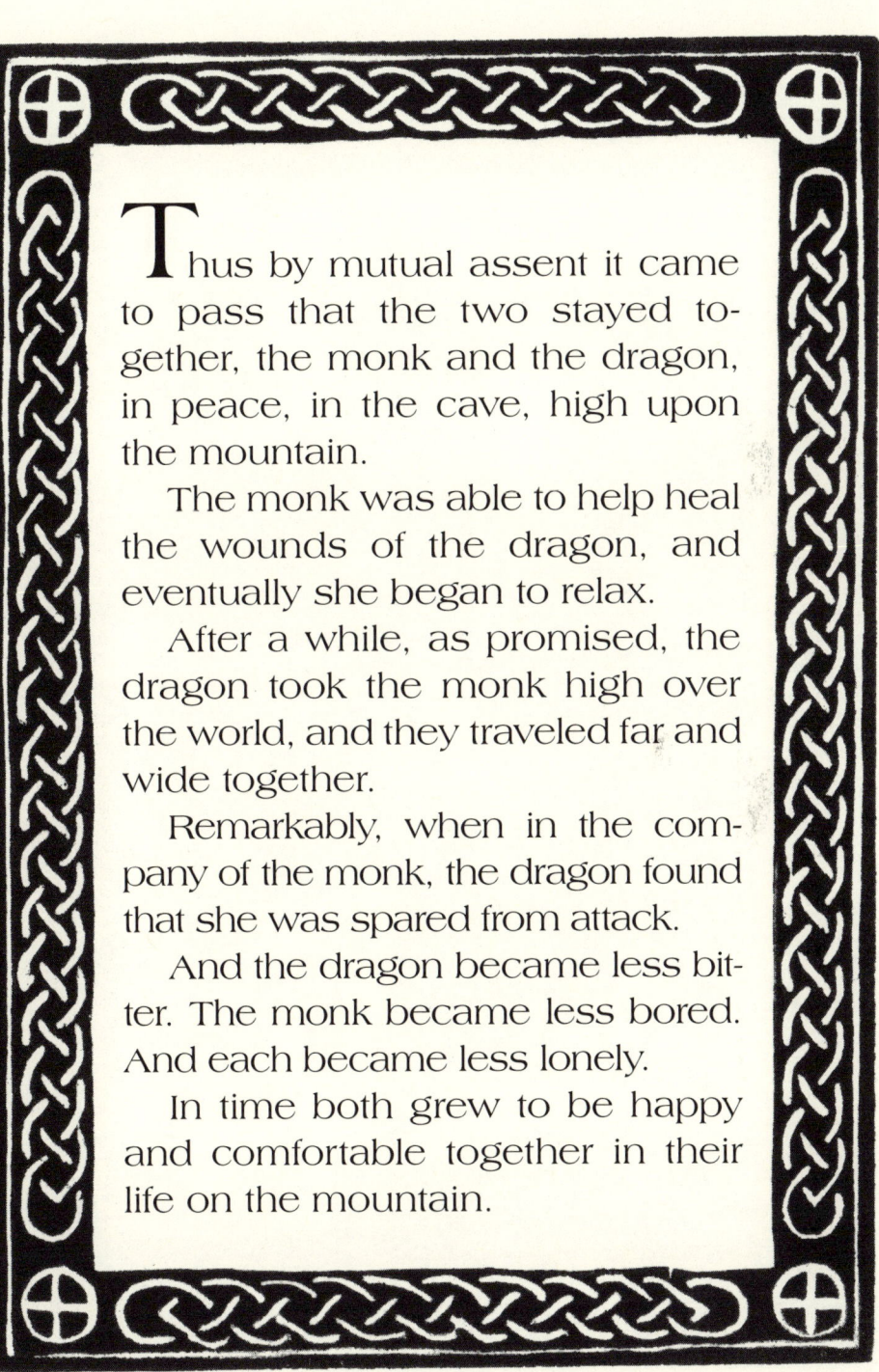

Thus by mutual assent it came to pass that the two stayed together, the monk and the dragon, in peace, in the cave, high upon the mountain.

The monk was able to help heal the wounds of the dragon, and eventually she began to relax.

After a while, as promised, the dragon took the monk high over the world, and they traveled far and wide together.

Remarkably, when in the company of the monk, the dragon found that she was spared from attack.

And the dragon became less bitter. The monk became less bored. And each became less lonely.

In time both grew to be happy and comfortable together in their life on the mountain.

But comfort permits an easing into old ways.

The monk began to spend more time alone, deep in the cave where the dragon couldn't reach him, and she was hurt by his neglect.

The dragon, in turn, began to dream furtively of faraway lands, and perceiving her distraction the monk felt excluded from her reveries.

At times they would argue, and with angry breath the dragon burned the monk on a few occasions.

This in turn earned his reproach and drove the monk deeper into his cave.

There came one cruel winter day when the monk would not come out at all, no matter how the dragon pleaded, stomped, or bellowed.

Finally exasperated, and with a last virago blast of fiery breath into the cave, the dragon flew up off the mountain and away from the cave leaving it behind smoldering.

As her silhouette passed into the distance, the mountain returned once again to the way it had been before her arrival — quiet and still.

The monk then returned to his lonely meditation, and the dragon to her solitary wandering.

But for the monk, solitude had lost its sweetness, and the tranquility of the past eluded him.

And for the dragon, faraway lands had lost their luster, and she found herself perpetually restless.

Neither could find the peace or joy that they'd both had together on the mountain, no matter how hard they tried.

In their separation, each began to quietly long for the other's company once again.

Finally it became too much to bear.

The monk, having become outwardly desperate, resolved to come down from the mountain in order to find the dragon.

The dragon, having wearied again of the world, decided to return in hope to the monk.

Each then set off to find the other.

However things went badly for the monk.

Away from the mountain he became lost, and in his naivety he found himself set upon by thieves — beaten, stabbed, and robbed of what little he had.

Wounded and left to die, the monk despaired of ever seeing his beloved dragon again.

As chance would have it, though, in her winged approach to the mountain, the dragon spied him from on high laying at the side of the road: cold, bleeding, and bewildered.

In great distress the dragon fell from the sky to where the monk lay, carefully lifted him up, and bore him hastily back to the mountain.

There she laid him down in the cave, warmed him with the heat of her breath, and gently bound his wounds.

Eventually, life began to return to the monk, and the dragon felt a great relief as she watched him quietly fall asleep.

Yet the dragon's outrage at the monk's assault would not be bound nor put to rest.

In a wrathful paroxysm she rose up off the mountain in a fury, cast herself in a blaze upon the sky, and went hunting the bandits down.

Finding them at camp in the night, the dragon fell upon them, sudden from out of the dark, and in a merciless rage she slaughtered them to a man in a fiery frenzy.

Once her fervor had been quelled, the dragon regarded the devastation she had wrought.

Unexpectedly she herself became overwhelmed by horror and ruth.

Utterly wearied, she turned away in shame and made her way heavily back to the mountain.

There the dragon found the monk on the threshold of the cave, awake, alert, and anxiously awaiting her return.

When she landed, she burst into anguished tears, imploring, "I do not ever want to leave this mountain again."

The monk held her tenderly, and with penitent tears welling in his own eyes he whispered, "I am so sorry. It was all my fault. We need not ever leave."

He then added, "But if ever I do venture away from this mountain again, you can be certain that I will always want you with me."

T hus it was that they again lived together, the monk and the dragon, in happiness upon the mountain.

Their days were joyful and filled with playful repartee, animated intercourse, and quiet dialogue.

In time they did venture anew into the faraway exotic lands of the world and enjoyed great adventure, but always in the end they came home together.

And there they stayed in each other's company, in peace, within in the cave, high upon the mountain, till the end of days.

Ω

Afterward

This is a fable. It is a true story. All good fables are true; otherwise, they wouldn't be good. It's also a love story unlike any you may have read before. It's our love story. By most measures our love is like many others. Yet to the two of us it is everything. Perhaps it's in that everything and in its very commonality that there may be something here for everyone.

We were inexplicably drawn to each other. It would be hubris to try to explain it. For both there was just something about the other that fascinated, something mysterious. When we began to date it was bliss.

But as any relationship grows there come disagreements, and so it was with ours. Somehow the forces that had drawn us together evolved into forces that drove us apart. This too was inexplicable. We came to an impasse. It seemed hopeless at times. We needed help.

We found it in writing. Eveline began a written conversation between us. Through texting, emails, and written letters we reapproached each other. Eveline realized she was temperamental, often feeling her words were misunderstood. She became frustrated and started to throw out angry words like flames that could burn. When John was confronted with or could not understand her words nor how to express his own feelings, he became withdrawn, a recluse.

So the story unfolded with Eveline identifying herself as a dragon and John as a monk. It is through this metaphor that self-realization occurred, and we came to relate to each other and each other's world. Through this imagery we learned a new way to speak with each other, how we could communicate, and how we could each learn to heal within ourselves but also come together.

What you hold in your hands is a result of that effort. It was born of the maelstrom of our ardent work together and things discovered therein. It came out of the deep mysteries of the human heart that welled up within our own particular selves and in our own small corner of the world. It is thus not a fantasy. It is true. It's as true as love.

John and Eveline Clark are married and have two grown children. John works as a physician and Eveline has a PhD in metaphysics. Reading, writing, and illustrating stories is their lifelong passion.